Lilac Haze

A COLLECTION OF SHORT STORIES AND FLASH FICTION

Shannon James

For Mum,
the most badass woman who ever lived and who I admire and love each and everyday

RITUAL

Sleep evades me. I shut my eyes, trapping my mind in darkness. Soon, the brief release from the loud, hissing thoughts will come.

It doesn't.

There is no slip into the slumbering shadows. No stillness. No silence.

Only the barrage of ceaseless fire forcing me to toss and turn.

Remember that one time you tried to be funny and nobody laughed? Pathetic-

I can't believe you made that conversation all about you. Self-absorbed much? Maybe next time be a better frie-

I snatch my phone from the bedside table and scroll mindlessly through the sea of socials, soaking in the numbness.

It never lasts long.

My eyes begin to drop before fully closing as I snuggle into the duvet, giving into the pull of sleep.

But its grip isn't strong enough and the bullets hail - hard and fast.

Remember when you fell and cried-

It's hilarious that you think they l-

You're so useless. Look at the time-

Everyone thinks you're a lo-

I groan loudly into the dark, halting the parasitic parts of my head for a moment.

'Fuck it,' I think. 'Let's just daydream instead…'

DÉJÀ VU

It wasn't my best decision to take the old dirt path. There was a reason for the danger sign sitting atop the wooden gateway. But I had climbed that gate today without a second glance.

Clambering over fallen trees and half-buried stones, I watched my feet carefully as one misstep could cause harm. Yet my mind continued to wander to my humiliation. The words, the laughter, the punches; it replayed like a never-ending tape, always rewinding back to the exact moment I had broken.

I forced myself to keep walking, knowing each step took me further away.

A strange atmosphere crept into the woodland. While the trees still hid me, their canopies blocking out the greying sky, the path suddenly forked in two with each way leading deeper. An invisible thread tugged me towards the left, where the land became vaguely familiar.

'You need to leave,' a low voice said into my ear. I turned, but my head began to ache and my vision blurred.

'Who's there?' Everything went dark as my eyes clasped shut.

'We need to get out of here,' the voice insisted. 'It's not safe.'

My eyes opened to see a familiar figure with auburn waves stood in front of me. She stared with glassy eyes and my sister took a step towards me.

'But I want to explore some more.' My laughter echoed through the woods as I took off down the left pathway.

'No, come back! You're going to get hurt!' The voice was faraway now. I smiled, climbing and jumping over the forest obstacles until my foot snagged under a rogue root. It shot me, like an arrow, straight into a tree.

I awoke back at the crossroads, balancing against a gnarled trunk. My eyes widened once the haze passed. She had left me again.

CALL OF THE WOODS

The bitter winds will turn anyone towards the woods. Lydia stopped for a moment to marvel at the sight. She was in no rush to get home since Mum and Dad would only be arguing again.

A canopy of fire rustled gently, entrancing her eyes. Leaves of orange, yellow and brown fell in slow, swirling motions. A small smile tugged at her lips as she watched the symphony of elements.

The wind blew harder, making her shiver. Even bundled up in all her knitted garments - there was no protection from the cold's icy pricks. The woods began to look inviting with its shelter and warmth.

Branches beckoned her closer. She took one step off the cobbled path leading home. The wind howled for her to keep going. It wasn't safe out in the open.

Another step cemented her decision. I won't stay long, she thought, just until the wind dies down. Her parents wouldn't even notice she was gone.

The ember leaves were falling more radically the closer she got. Twisting around her, but never quite touching the ground. The wind had them meandering in a way that blocked her off from the outside. She didn't look back anyway, walking further and further into her new home.

Never answer the call of the woods.

THE DISAPPOINTMENT

'You were meant to restore our reputation!' my father bellowed. 'You were meant to restore me-us, to the pinnacle of high society!'

The same speech. The same parading around the room with hands on his hips. The same red, pudgy face spitting saliva and words at me. Oh, how this had become my favourite entertainment recently. I cocked my chair back with a smirk.

'You forgot about the part where this will hang over the family for generations to come.' That set him off on his next tirade. I never really listened. None of what he spoke meant anything to me - the prestige, fame, money.

My mother slumped in her black leather chair, weeping at my destitute future. At least it would be a happy one, I thought.

Meanwhile, my father carried on his moaning about how much of a disappointment I was to the noble name of Ashton.

I laughed at the irony. He was the reason they had fallen from favour with the Gods of snobbery at that damn country club. One insulting joke by him had ostracised them. He believed my betrayal would only solidify his new social standing.

'It won't be funny when I cut you off.' He'd reached his big finale. The vein in his forehead was close to bursting from his skin. He looked expectantly at me with a scowl. It was hilarious how he thought this time his tantrum would make me fall in line like one of his employees.

'Do it then,' I said before getting up to walk away. I tuned out the ramblings of how I'll be sorry and I need him. Always the same speech.

I put on my headphones and went out into the fresh breeze of spring. Tension evaporated from my body immediately. A faint sigh escaped my lips. All this anger just because I decided to become an artist.

SNOW FALL

The snow began to fall this evening. Translucent flakes of white drifting to the ground and melting into nothing. I watched from the warmth of the kitchen window.

Flakes turned into sleet and hurtled towards the earth, battering the frozen ground. From graceful ballet to frenzied tango in a handful of moments.

It changed the landscape white into a blank canvas. A fresh start. It even covered the new grave I dug behind the rose beds. That gave me more time. I turned the taps off, letting the murky red water drain away.

ONE WORD

'Wow, you're such an idiot,' Clara jokes, leading to giggles from us all.

Idiot. My laughter becomes hollow and distant. *Idiot.* The word burns deep into my head, leaving a smouldering mess of panic behind.

It's only a joke, I think, no need to spiral over nothing. *Idiot.* But that slither of doubt that it's not erases all rationality.

'All jokes have truth in them,' the voice whispers. 'This is what they really think of you.'

That's not true, I think, it's just-

'You know I'm right,' it snarls. 'You're an idiot and they're all laughing about it.'

I bury my nails into the skin under my jumper. The pain distracts me momentarily from the venom of the voice. *Idiot.* It roars louder as the voice feeds the flames. There's no escape or distraction. All I can do is keep on laughing alongside them.

SONDER

Water dripped from my face as I sprinted through the rainy streets of the town centre. I dodged between the crowds of shoppers, weaving from street to street, tightly gripping the stack of boxes in my arms. The rusted signs of the run-down shops passed by me in a dull blur.

Dark grey clouds, the same dull colour as my eyes, floated leisurely across the sky. Shaking my head, I stared straight ahead. Rain continued to pound against the cobbled pavement, causing me to slip every so often.

'Shit,' I said under my breath as I nearly crashed to the ground. The boxes began to fall before I regained my footing. Shifting their weight back into the middle of my arms, I glanced at my watch. It was nearly one o'clock. 'Shit.'

I broke off back into a sprint. The rain pelted straight into me, soaking through my green jacket and into the clothes underneath. Small droplets of water dribbled down my arms and chest as my t-shirt became utterly drenched. Cold ruptured its way through me like a glaciating lake. I grimaced, berating myself for leaving the giant umbrella and parka coat by the door.

The entire morning had been nothing but shambles. Because my stupid alarms had been snoozed, I woke up ten minutes before I needed to leave. This was then followed by a clumsy show of me picking up whatever clothes were nearest and becoming tangled in them, while I tried to brush my teeth simultaneously. Because of all that, my t-shirt was on inside out under the jacket, I was wearing odd socks and I didn't even put a bra on. To end it all off, I had fallen down the stairs, trying to grab the boxes on the way down before darting out the door without even a goodbye to my parents.

It felt like the universe had some sort of vendetta against me at the moment. Everything kept going wrong. I had failed my last essay at university, so I was going to have to redo that at some point. Some guy I had been seeing for the last three months had ghosted me out of nowhere. I kept being late for work, my car had broken down and my phone had been waterboarded by the toilet. To top it all off, my older brother was in the hospital after a car had smashed into him on his motorbike.

There was some luck left though as he had escaped the accident with only a few broken ribs, some nasty bruises and cuts and an inflated ego from being waited on by everyone. I would roll my eyes and complain when he kept asking for me to refill his water cup, put his phone on charge or read to him. But I really didn't mind doing them. They were small tasks, and it made his stay in the hospital a little easier, especially after everything he had been through.

The side street widened as I caught sight of the main road and the cars racing past. I grinned and glimpse at my watch. It was only eight minutes past one. The bus wasn't due for another four minutes. Taking a deep breath, I pushed my legs faster.

Throwing myself around the corner onto the main street, I searched for the bus stop and locked onto it.

There was no bus in sight yet.

Before I could rejoice, I slammed into something that sent me hurtling to the ground. The boxes went flying in all directions as the back of me hit the wet pavement below. I groaned in frustration, plopping myself up onto my elbows. A teenage boy lay in front of me, rubbing his head.

'You need to watch where you're going,' I snapped before pushing myself up. My back was soaked and half of my tangled hair had fallen out of the very messy bun. I quickly scrapped it back, but a few blonde stragglers clung to my face.

'I'm so sorry,' the boy said, getting up onto his feet unsteadily. 'You came out of nowhere! I'm really sorry, miss!' He scurried to the left of me to pick up a skateboard. I raised an eyebrow and the boy looked away sheepishly.

No wonder he had collided with me. His mind would've been elsewhere. No self-awareness, like most teenagers.

The young man tugged at his sleeve as I looked him over. He wore a faded grey army jacket, ripped jeans and a beanie hat that just about covered his ginger curls. I sighed, glancing in front of me. A bus was pulling into the stop.

'Shit! That's my bus.' I began frantically looking around for the boxes. One was in a puddle, the other by my feet and the last one on a bench by the boy. Whilst quickly grabbing the box at my feet, I spun on my heel and dived for the one in the puddle. I ignored the drenched cardboard and the fact it was beginning to fall apart. That was something to figure out later. I juggled the boxes between my hands, trying to haul the least soaked one to the top.

The doors of the bus screeched opened.

'Excuse me, miss?' The boy tugged at the back of my jacket and I whirled around, gritting my teeth to hold my tongue. He shrunk away, but kept his hands outstretched, offering me the last box. My face softened as guilt crept in.

An apology was forming when I opened my mouth to speak, but suddenly the screeching of the bus doors began again. Quickly, I grabbed the box from the boy and smiled.

'Thank you so much,' I blurted out before turning and racing towards the bus, waving frantically. The doors stopped and started opening up again. Catching my breath at my mad dash, I looked back at the child. He still stood in the same spot, smiling shyly. The warmth of gratitude tugged at my heart. I gave the boy a quick smile and wave before he disappeared from view. Jumping on the bus, I plonked myself in the first seat I saw after getting my ticket and let out a sigh of relief.

The bus jutted forward.

While the two driest boxes sat on the seat at my side, the drenched one stayed firmly on my knee. Only the bottom of it had been completely soaked through. I opened the box, silently praying that the wrapping inside had protected the contents.

Six chocolate cupcakes greeted me, still intact. I gave a little squeal at the realisation I hadn't ruined anything. Everything would go to plan and be perfect for my brother's welcome home party.

Keeping the box steady, I glanced around the bus. It was quiet for a Friday afternoon and there were five of us spread out between the tattered, fraying seats.

A woman and child sat across from me with a tower of bags filled with clothes and food. The child was chatting away happily as the woman smiled and nodded. But her tired eyes looked faraway. An older man with a tartan green cap and grey coat sat in the middle of the bus, grumbling away at the newspaper he read. And at the back, a young woman sat with a dirty blue gym bag. She caught my eye and scowled before shoving her hood up to hide her face.

I spun back around, shrinking into the seat. Guilt flushed my cheeks, as I remembered the way I had reacted towards the boy from before. There was no excuse other than I was blindsided by the urgency of catching this bus. It hadn't even crossed my mind to think about the boy, other than that he had slowed me down.

Yet, he could've been rushing somewhere too. Or just out for some fresh air. I'd never know because it wasn't my life.

I poked my head around the bus again. These people had their own stories they were living. They all had days that were bad, happy or boring. Everyone was living or battling through something. I sighed, resting my head against the rumbling window.

MASQUERADE

The masquerade began at seven. Nobody was permitted in without a mask. I watched as everyone became a stranger, hiding their real selves behind disguise.

The girl enchanting the room with charisma in her intricate, golden veil was normally the introvert who stayed home on the weekends. And the usually timid one, now adorned with the classic comedy mask, captivated the crowd with jokes.

I wore the mask with the joker-like smile to trick my peers too, bouncing between conversations. Yet, the sadness was still consuming me, even with my false laughter.

LONG JOURNEY HOME

The time-worn gentleman prepared for his last journey. On went the tweed flat cap along with the matching trench coat. Rain clouds were gathering outside the window in a hoard of misery. He grabbed the black umbrella, while the greyed spaniel waited patiently at the door. Patrick kissed his wife before she joined him by the hand.

Opening the door to a dulling world, Patrick decided they would go left instead of right today. The rows of terraced houses he passed stood tall, like urbanised trees, as Alfie bounced ahead. Cars stormed past. Weather-proofed people clambered to get inside. Yet Patrick took no notice. His eyes focused, pinpointing his route. He led them into the pathway of a small church.

'I love coming back here,' he said with an affectionate smile. 'Sixty years and it hasn't changed since the day I married you.'

The wild daffodils shone, guiding him like the hidden sun. They danced in the wind around Patrick like they had many years ago when he had danced with them. These were always her favourites. He plucked a dozen of them and joined them together with a yellow ribbon.

Alfie lay by a marble grave, where he whimpered at Patrick. The daffodils were placed gently on the head, where Patrick's hand traced the carved words of 'beloved wife'. He shed a tear as the sky began to weep with him.

'I miss her too,' Patrick sighed, placing a hand on Alfie's head while he stared at the picture that never left his hand.

EIRENE

The frothy aftermath of the waves surged their way towards the child sitting and waiting. She squealed with joy once again when the water soaked her. Yet it left as quickly as it came. Frowning, she tried to wade in deeper, causing an explosion of splashes. A hand caught her and laughed.

'I swear you're part fish,' her mother said, 'but stay where it's safe. The sea can be dangerous.'

The girl nodded and remained by her side for now. But the allure of the glistening ocean, like a sapphire in the sun, made the warning drown beneath the happy memories. It became a tradition for the girl to be the last out, dripping wet and grinning. Her family joked she must be descended from Poseidon. She only smirked before running back to her domain.

Nobody noticed she waded further in every new summer, exploring the depths forbidden to her. She wanted to find dolphins, colourful fish or even treasure. She knew these weren't in the shallows.

The ocean always protected her, keeping her head above the water when she no longer reached the bottom. It then returned her to the muddy sand where her parents waited. Until one day, it claimed her.

Her grieving parents still wait by the shoreline. They call her name, ignoring the stares and pitying looks. Their little girl will return one day as long as they wait.

MARK OF VICTORY

Walking into the old brick pub made me instinctively put a hand over my pocket with my wallet and keys in. The floors were sticky and had fragments of broken glass scattered around the edges. Grey paint coated all the walls, chipped and faded. Mismatched chairs gathered around stained tables. For midday, the pub was lively, with booming laughter and shouting deafening the ears.

I had only come in here to grab a quick drink while I waited for my car to have its MOT. Normally, I always get my MOT a month earlier than expected to be on the safe side. But this time it had completely slipped my mind until I saw an ad for cheap ones on my phone yesterday. My eyes had widened as the realisation that my MOT was nearly due hit me. In hasty fashion, I had begun ringing every garage in a twenty-mile radius and one had miraculously fit me in today.

They had told me to come back in a couple of hours to check in. With time to burn and a throat to quench, I walked into the first bar establishment I saw. And that's how I ended up in this dingy place called The White Hart.

I halted at the entrance as I took in the surroundings and the smell of must, sweat and beer smacked me right in the face. Forcing myself to hold back a gag, I started debating whether to just go to the corner shop to get a drink and sit on a bench somewhere.

'What you havin'?' the bartender shouted from across the room. Internally, I groaned as I locked eyes with him. He was a tall man with shaven, brown hair wearing the all black uniform. An eyebrow piercing glinted in the dim light while he continued polishing a pint glass, waiting for my answer.

Plastering a small smile on my face, I strode over to the bar. There was no way I could leave now without being rude, and that wasn't the way I was raised. I slipped onto a barstool and mumbled an order for a pint of lemonade with extra ice. The bartender gave me a bemused look before attending to my order.

Two men were sitting next to me and were engaged in a boisterous conversation about the current habits of penguins. I looked over, pretending to adjust my glasses. The one in my direct eye-line looked relatively normal with dark, messy hair that he wore short. His clothing was a tattered green jumper paired with jeans and black trainers. The only feature that was out of the ordinary was a jagged scar slashed along his cheek.

'What ya lookin' at?' the man snarled. 'My mark of victory?'

'No, I was just-'

He stood up and pushed his way into my face, wedging me between him and the wooden bar. His mouth curled into a smirk as he put an arm around me.

'Well, since ya so nosy, I'll tell ya how I got it.' His voice turned light-hearted as he took the seat next to me. His friend sighed, turning around to join us. He seemed younger than the other one, with floppy blond hair and a baby face full of freckles. The complete opposite to my own curly, dark hair and stubbled face.

'Honestly, it's fine. I don't want-'

'Bout a year ago, I was walkin' home from this very pub bout midnight, I know… early for me, when I decided to take a shortcut through an alley,' he began. 'Now, everyone round here knows not to take that alley. Bad reputation, ya know? But when you're on the lash. I was bout halfway down when they jumped me.'

He had somehow gathered the attention of the whole pub. Every patron watched him, laughing and shaking their heads. Lavishing in the attention, our storyteller jumped up from his stool and began acting out the next part.

'There were five, nah, six guys and I knew the only way I was getting out of this was with my fists.' He raised his fists, showing off his hairy knuckles, before he started punching his imaginary assailants. 'I took 'em all on and would have won if one of the little shits didn't have a knife.'

Silence. Scar-face took a deep breath and pointed to his cheek, 'He sunk it straight into 'ere.'

Next came the theatrics of how he had still managed to scare off these kids while bleeding profusely.

His friend leant over to me and whispered, 'This is utter bullshit, ya know. He really got it from fallin' into that table over there pissed.'

THE FOX IN THE CITY

A pair of amber eyes locked with mine across the street. The artificial light painted their orange fur fluorescent as it stopped in the spotlight. A fox come to scavenge in the big city, hidden from man by the illusion of night. Always safe because of their slyness.

Teach me, I begged silently; I want to be unafraid to walk these wild streets.

Their only response was to vanish into the dark alley. Another swig of whiskey burned my lips as I purged myself of him.

THE LITTLE THINGS

The small child flashed into the room as quick as the crack of lightning that splintered the sky. Lucy buried her head in the crumpled duvet. The covers enshrouded her, becoming a cocoon of protection against the explosions about to start. On cue, thunder boomed and echoed in the distance, creeping closer to the cottage every time.

Lucy let out a high shrick and clambered onto her slumbering mother. Her hands were vices against her mother's skin, clamping down hard over her waist, digging her nails in.

Her mother jolted awake and before she could even open her blurry eyes, Lucy threw herself into her arms.

'What's wrong, sweetheart?' the mother asked, wrapping her arms around her trembling child. The next flash of lightning that lit the room answered for Lucy, and her mother held her closer. 'It's only a storm, it'll pass don't worry.'

The soothing words did nothing for Lucy as she clutched her mother tighter, bracing herself for the next round of thunder.

More roaring in the sky came, but it was getting too close. A sob escaped from the child's throat. Each new roar was an ominous countdown.

'You know, the thunder ponies must be busy tonight to be making all that noise,' her mother said.

The child stared up into the pale blue eyes that mirrored her own and titled her head in confusion. 'The thunder ponies?'

'Yes, the thunder ponies! That's what's making all the racket up there. Gosh, they must be having some fun and galloping about. What do you think?'

Lucy paused for a moment, imagining the grey steeds frolicking about amongst the clouds, their hooves sending thunder to the earth.

More thunder boomed as if it was directly over them, causing Lucy to flinch.

'They must be galloping away now,' her mother mused, 'they never stay in the same place for long. Wait and see.'

Lucy waited, conjuring image after image of these mystical horses chasing each other or playing tag. It's not their fault that their feet cause thunder, Lucy thought, they're only trying to have fun.

Another clap of thunder came, but as her mother predicted, it was receding into the distance away from the cottage.

'See,' her mother smiled, tucking Lucy under her arm as she lay on the bed. 'Now tell me, what games do you think they were playing?'

For years after the creation of the thunder ponies, Lucy would always jump into her mother's bed during a storm to talk about these mischievous horses. It would soothe her enough that she wasn't so frightened the next time they visited.

Even at twenty years old when a storm hits, Lucy still feels the familiar calm her mother eased into her thanks to the thunder ponies.

ON THE DOORSTEP

One day, I snapped. Grabbing my keys and driving away from the colourless walls of that office helped nothing. My paranoid mind went into overdrive instead. Question after question threw themselves at me. *Would I be fired? Was it time for a change? What about all the bills coming up?*

I looked out of my window for a distraction and found the welsh countryside staring back. Pulling over, my mouth became agape. Jagged mountains laced with viridian surrounded me. Specks of white roamed the mountainside in the safety of their muted-grey pens. The road ran with the inclines like nature's own rollercoaster. And a lilac haze covered the mounts in the distance, making me believe it went on forever.

The sight awoke something primal in me. All I wanted to do was wander the wild lands of Wales and discover more of these awe-striking views.

For years, this beauty had become a backdrop to my everyday stress after the initial enchantment of living in rural Wales faded. It had remained unnoticed, unappreciated like artwork hidden away in a vault. No more, I thought, getting back in the car before driving off further into the valleys.

C'EST LA VIE

My legs buckled from under me as I clutched the rough bark of a tree for support. A faint thud echoed through the forest. I let out a ragged breath, sliding down the tree. The navy torch I had been holding a moment ago laid beside me. It cast a soft glow into a section of the dark forest, illuminating some of the tall trees. It was like a lighthouse to those who were lost in the sea of darkness. Except it was only me that was lost.

I lifted a shaky hand towards my shoulder as I tried to remove my backpack from behind. It took several clumsy attempts, but eventually I tugged the pack free and shoved it into my lap. My head lulled against the tree as the dizziness set in. My hands went limp at my sides. And my mouth opened and closed like a fish dying on dry land.

Water. That was all I needed. Just a drop of cold water to get rid of the desert in my mouth.

I forced my head down to look at the backpack. One step at a time, I told myself. Slowly, my hands rose to unzip the pack and fumble inside to find the bottle of water. As soon as the cool metal brushed my fingertips, I snatched it straight out of the bag, ripping the lid off.

The bottle halted itself above my thrown-back head, halting my urge to douse myself in the refreshing liquid. I needed to ration it. With the uncertainty of my situation, I couldn't afford to waste my only supply for one moment of relief.

I shoved my head forward and forced myself to take a tiny sip from the bottle. As I swallowed, the water was a tsunami crashing through my throat, bringing it back to life.

Leaning back against the tree, I let a small sigh and closed my eyes. I knew that small drop of so-called salvation wouldn't rid me of the dehydration, but it would buy me some time. The only way I was surviving this ordeal was by finding the way out of this forest.

So far, the exit had eluded me. The further I had travelled into the sprawling land of woodlands, the more the landscape had become one of the same. Endless trees in every direction.

My breathing slowed, my energy fading like the long-gone sunlight. A sensation of fatigue pooled in my muscles. It wouldn't hurt to rest for a while. I cracked open my eyes. Total darkness had enveloped the forest now. Including me.

The torch must of finally died, I thought. My foggy brain tried to make out the shadowy shapes in my line of vision, but it all just blended into the night.

Yet, the forest was alive. Far off owls hooted to each other, while closer by the scurry of smaller creatures echoed faintly into the trees. A small breeze rustled the leaves. More distorted sounds that my brain couldn't place joined the mixture of noise to create a nocturnal lullaby. Tiredness tugged at me, pulling me into a deep sleep.

A soft chirping rang through my ears as the clutches of sleep began to release their grip. Tossing myself over to the other side of my rock hard bed made no difference in getting rid of the noise. I let out a groan before opening my eyes, only slightly, to a bright new day. A slice of sunlight stabbed into my vision. I squinted, moving my hand to rub my eyes as they adjusted to the new daylight.

My arms stretched slightly as I wondered how long I'd been out for. Alarms began blaring in my head as I stopped mid stretch. Too long, my parched throat warned. I had only meant to rest for a while, only enough to recuperate some energy. Yet, the blinding light of the sun was a testament to all the hours I had lost.

Panic overtook as I scrambled to find my bottle.

It was a constant cycle. The need for water, but never having enough. Then, the dehydration feeding the fatigue that caused me to lose so many precious hours. I knew I couldn't keep this up much longer. I knew my body was slowly failing. I knew time was no longer a luxury I had.

My hand grasped the bottle and went straight for the lid. A waterfall gushed, tumbling right into my mouth. Relief surged through my throat as the cool water flooded it.

In a moment of dreaded realisation, I forced the bottle away from me. The last dregs of water dripped out.

'No, no, no, what have I done?' I whispered, staring at the empty bottle as if it might automatically fill back up. I was on borrowed time. Either I needed to find my way out now or at least find more water. A string of curse words left my lips as I attempted to scramble up.

'Leaving so soon?' a husky voice called out in front of me. I stopped mid-motion, frozen to the spot.

In all my time being lost in this forest, I had encountered nobody.

A shiver ran down my spine.

I closed my eyes and counted to three before I slowly turned my head to find the owner. The sun continued to blind me as I raised my hand to block the rays.

'Who's there?' I asked in a shaky voice.

'Your saviour,' the voice said. A figure materialised from the tree-line, the sunlight lining their silhouette making them glow. I revered at the sight of the luminous figure, falling to my knees. Was I hallucinating, I thought, or was my luck finally turning?

As the figure edged closer, their features started to reveal themselves. Pale blue eyes, like the winter sky, bore into me as the figure stopped a few inches in front of me. The man, who towered high above me, looked down and smiled. It was an inviting smile, one that blunted his sharp features. Yet, there was a harshness in his face that caused me to recoil from him. There was something too perfect, too beautiful about the stranger, as if he had been carved by the heavens.

'Who are you?' I set my mouth into a firm line.

The stranger's smile never faltered. 'I told you, I'm your saviour.'

'That doesn't answer my question.'

The man let out a low chuckle that seemed to boom through the woodland. A strand of his slicked back, platinum hair fell over his face. He pushed it back in place. 'Does it matter who I am?' He shook his head, still smiling. 'I would think that all you cared for was surviving this terrible ordeal and that my help would be appreciated.'

I bit my lip at his offer as I turned it over in my mind. My situation was dire. No water, food or time. The only hope I had on my own was to find water before I finally succumbed to the dehydration. And that was only a slim hope. But this person was a complete stranger who had appeared out of nowhere.

With a quick glance, I noted the immaculate appearance of the man. There was not one hair or piece of clothing out of place on him. He wore a white cotton shirt accompanied by a silken, midnight blue waistcoat. The sleeves of the shirt were rolled up to his forearms, displaying the lean muscles in them. His shirt was tucked into a pair of formal black trousers and the waistcoat hung unbuttoned around his frame. There was an air of casual elegance that emanated from the stranger.

Yet, this pristine form was a cause of concern. There was no plausible explanation for someone to look the way he did after wandering the woods.

I thought of my appearance in comparison. The last time I had gazed at myself was in the reflection of a quiet brook and I hadn't even recognised the dishevelled woman staring at me. The dull brown plait hung limply over my shoulder in a greasy, dry mess. There seemed to be more hair outside of the plait than in it. Heavy, dark circles sat beneath the sunken eyes. Cracks permeated along my lips like the aftershock of an earthquake, with the skin deciding to collapse in on itself. I was a walking corpse.

That had been a few days ago. I cringed to think what I must look like now. Near-death was all that came to mind.

While lost in my thoughts, the stranger had taken up residence opposite my tree, lounging leisurely in the sun a few metres away from me. I fell back against the rough bark, beginning to feel the strain of kneeling. A sharp pain shot through my legs. I let out a short groan that brought the stranger's attention back to me.

'So, have you thought about my offer? You seemed lost for a minute there.'

I scowled at him. This only caused him to smile wider in amusement. He seemed to take some pleasure from my misery, adding further confusion to the enigma of him.

There was something ugly hidden beneath this man that made every nerve inside of me scream not to trust him.

But I had no other options.

'How can you even help?' I sighed.

'With this for a start.' He chucked a bottle in my direction. It landed with a thud at my side, the bare silver shining in the sun, identical to my own. I slowly reached for it, not breaking eye contact with him. It felt heavy in my hands. I gave it a hesitant shake. Liquid sloshed inside. A small gasp escaped from my dried lips. It was full of something and my throat screamed for it to be water.

'Go ahead,' the stranger smiled, nodding towards the bottle. 'It's all yours.'

I twisted the lid off and brought the bottle to the barest inch of my mouth before a troubled thought leaked its way into my head. What if it's poisoned, a small voice said. I shut the voice down, beyond cautiousness at this point. Whatever this liquid was, it didn't matter anymore. I couldn't help myself anymore, so if this stranger wanted to poison me here and now, at least it would be a quick death.

I took a massive gulp, feeling the same relief from the cool water as every time before. My eyes locked back on the man, his pale gaze searching mine. I waited for several moments, waiting for any signs of poison, waiting for death. He tilted his head, confusion clouding his features, causing the smile to fade. I held his stare, my expression remaining stony.

A smirk appeared on his face as he rose to his feet. He stood at his full height over me, offering a hand. 'Do you trust me now?'

My wariness of the stranger persisted. Much of what was happening made no sense, but I was so drained. All I knew was that I just wanted to leave this forest. My hand wrapped around his, cementing my need for his help. Even though he had proven trustworthy so far, I just couldn't let go of the unease.

He pulled me up, my legs shaking beneath me.

'Steady,' his voice whispered in my ear. 'Just lean into me.'

My remaining strength seeped from me as I let my whole body fall into him. He led me a little way into the forest until he stopped us in the middle of a more open woodland area. The towering trees circled around, providing only flecks of sunlight that broke through the cage of their canopies. A gentle trickle of water hummed through the air, harmonising with the continuous chirping of the birds. I felt my body to relax for the first time in a while as the stranger guided me towards a fallen log. He held my arm as I slowly planted myself in the dirt with my back against the log. My tattered, dirty backpack dropped at my side as the man placed the bottle into my lap.

'Keep drinking,' he said. 'You need to start getting your strength up.'

I took another massive gulp, relishing in the cool liquid. With my thirst becoming quenched and my head clearer, I needed to start rationing the water again. It would help me in the future if or when I needed to make a quick getaway. I placed the water bottle at my side, giving it a slight shake. It sounded about half full. I let out a small sigh of relief.

'Feel better now?' I shot my eyes in the voice's direction and gave a quick nod. He was carrying an armful of twigs and leaves. A small smile appeared on his lips as he focused his attention on setting the foliage in a pile near the log. 'Good. I think it's time we finally talked about your precarious situation.'

'How you're going to help me, you mean?' I asked. That had been his offer. He'd proved helpful so far, but the atmosphere seemed to have turned more ominous. It could have been the cold tone he now spoke in or the way his smile seemed to be curving upwards menacingly, like the motion of someone raising a knife upward in preparation to stab.

'Something like that,' was all he replied before striding back towards the trees. My hand clenched around the water bottle. I tried propping myself further up on the log, just to see how much strength I'd regained.

Not enough, I thought bitterly, as I slid back, scowling at my incompetences.

Something wasn't right. There had been no reason for this stranger to help me, yet he had. He had provided me with water, temporary safety and support in my weakness. But the change of demeanour exposed him. He was playing some twisted game with me and I didn't want to stick around to find out.

I grunted, forcing myself up onto the log before placing my feet firmly on the ground. My eyes shut as the dizziness began to make everything whirl. It was better on the ground, but that just left me vulnerable.

Footsteps crunched under twigs. I jumped, whipping my head towards the sound.

It was only him, carrying bigger pieces of wood from fallen branches. But he was spinning. I groaned, shoving my head into my lap.

'Sorry, didn't mean to scare you,' he said in a breezy tone. 'Just want to get this fire done with before we get down to business.' I heard the clutter of branches dropping to the ground. The stranger began humming as he busied himself stomping around the log.

Suddenly, the noise stopped. The forest was quiet from human sound and was left to its own raucous. It would be smart to look, but I still felt nauseous from the dizziness. I bit my lip as anxiety twisted in my stomach. 'Why have you moved?' There was a hint of amusement in his voice. 'You'd feel better on the ground.'

'I can't stay on the ground forever,' I mumbled.

'I suppose.' More twigs snapped as I sensed the man stand. 'I'll be right back. Try to rest up for a moment.'

Like magic, his words seemed to make my limbs ache with tiredness. I tried to fight it, but it was a losing battle with my eyes already in darkness. Slowly, I gave in and shut down.

I woke up with a start, nearly falling off the log as another loud crackle lashed through the air. My hand clutched my chest and my eyes adjusted to the nighttime. A fire burned near me, giving the woodland an orange aura. The stranger sat opposite, his face luminous in the firelight, poking the fire with a stick as it let out some smaller crackles. He sat with his hand resting on his knee and the other leg sticking out.

'Look who finally woke up,' he grinned at me. 'Thought it would be nice for you to have some warmth.' I held my hands out towards the fire, basking in the heat it radiated. It soothed me into a smile for a moment. The warmth danced all over my skin, bathing me in another luxury I thought lost.

A sharp laugh cut through the silence. 'You must be feeling better after that nap.'

My scowl reappeared. 'It seems weird though since I wasn't even tired until you said.' Our eyes locked as I narrowed mine. 'Funny how words can have that effect on you.'

'Ah,' he smirked. 'You caught onto that then.'

'Who are you?' I held my stare, pushing my fear down. His eyes brightened, glowing like a blue flame. This person was no ordinary man. I tightened my grip around the bottle; it was my only weapon at this precise moment. It was time to end whatever was happening here, and begin unravelling his game.

'I have gone by many names over the centuries,' he began. 'Some have called me an angel, others a demon. Someone even once called me a witch.' He let out a slight chuckle at this revelation. 'But I have always preferred to be called Fate. Rolls off the tongue better.'

'You're…Fate?' I scrunched my face up in confusion. Fate had always been an otherworldly force, one that people would dismiss because it was beyond everyone's control. It was essentially the embodiment of c'est la vie - that's life; it was never a living, sentient entity.

'Something of that nature,' he shrugged.

'Then why are you here? Why are you bothering me?' I demanded in a desperate shriek, edging closer to the end of the log as his gaze burned into me. My throat was ash, dry and charred.

I had never believed in the supernatural and definitely didn't want their attention. My eyes darted into the tree-line beyond the orange glow, where darkness reigned. It felt safer than here.

'I have an offer for you,' he said, suddenly sensing my flightiness. He pulled out a silver coin and held it out flat in his hand. It was much bigger than an ordinary coin, fitting comfortably on his entire palm. There was a crescent moon imprinted on the side facing upwards. He turned the coin over to reveal the other side, as golden as the sun emblazoned on it. 'In a moment, I'm going to flip this and if it lands on the sun, you are free from this forest. You'll wake up back home and it'll be like this was all a horrifying nightmare.'

'Why would you help me?' The question came out as a plea. Fate didn't involve itself in its predetermined threads. It lets the events run, watching its masterpiece like any other audience; enjoying, but never intervening.

He ignored me. 'If it lands on the moon, then you get to spend eternity in the darkness.'

'What if I refuse?'

'There is no refusal. This is how your story plays out.' He flipped the coin into the air. It arched high, and I tried feebly to grab it, to change the events already unfolding. The coin began to make its descent as I fell hopelessly into the dirt. I watched as it fell into the twisting flames. I rushed to my knees to see the outcome, ignoring the burning heat.

A terrifying laugh echoed through the air as the flames turned silver. They coiled around me, suffocating my very being. A scream rose in my throat, but could not escape. The blazing heat snaked further around my body until I was entirely engulfed in flames. My eyes met with Fate's. He gave me one last smile before I succumbed to the darkness.

ABSENCE

The End.

Those words blazed in my mind, dragging me back to the reality of my bedroom, away from the world I yearned for until I was me again.

All that greeted me were the dimly lit pages of the book staring up at me. I blinked a few times; letting the hollowness set in. I could never lose myself in this world, these characters, this story for the first time again.

Longing clawed at me, rearing an ugly craving to escape back.

I sighed, knowing this void would last for days until I found a new world. Another fleeting story to distract myself from the horrors of existence. I strode over to the polished wood of my bookcase and grabbed another.

Once upon a time…

Shannon James

THE LOST KINGDOM

The sun had sunk below the country hills of the village. Night was spreading; infecting the land with a darkness, starting a deprivation of sight. As the starless sky turned charcoal, dots of light flickered on from the hills, like fireflies hovering in the distance.

I breathed in the cool night air through my open window. Everything was so silent. Closing my eyes, I breathed deeply once again, trying to let this atmospheric peace infest me. I breathed out, emptying my mind. A brief calm settled over me.

Yet, when I gazed back at the vastness and quiet of the landscape, all it did was remind me of how alone I was.

'Fuck it.' I threw the duvet over me, cocooning myself away.

The rustling leaves and snaps of twigs and branches caused me to fling the duvet across the room. Light exploded in the room as I flicked my lamp on. I glanced around frantically, but my room remained unchanged. The grey desk held my scattered drawings, unfinished college work and remnants of stationary and make up. Pieces of my clothing hung around the room, like decorations, in an array of black, burgundy, and deep purple. Some were on the back of my desk chair, the door and even the wardrobe handles. It was a mess, but it was my mess. One that would be sorted, eventually.

I turned away from the room as hushed voices came from the window. It was pure night now with no presence of the day before. The time on my phone read twenty-three minutes past eleven. Too late for anyone to be out in this place. Yet, the voices became braver as they got louder with laughter. Where was it coming from?

The voices seemed to carry from behind the garden, where a little woodland stood. The neglect it had faced over the years from overgrowth, fly-tipping and fallen trees had caused it to be bordered off with a fine for trespassers. Better to fence it off, the community had said, keep the hooligans out. That's how the den was lost.

My eyes widened as the realisation struck me. I knew where the voices were coming from. The old den. Someone had actually managed to find a way in.

The fences that guarded it were around ten feet tall, with nasty spikes atop each of the pickets. It lined the back of my garden since it had been installed over five years ago. Mum had hated how it ruined her pretty garden and had made dad build a bigger fence to cover it from view. Yet, it was always still visible from my window.

I pushed myself further out into the cool air, straining to listen to the voices. They were loud and carefree, but there were too many of them. Each strand of sound became tangled together. A garbled mess echoing into the night.

Sinking back into my pillow, I huffed. There was a way in. After all these years, I could finally go back.

In silence, I crept towards the door. As it opened slowly, I grabbed the black jacket hanging from the doorknob and slipped it on. The house was eerily quiet. Even my parents' breathing was a shallow sound murmuring in the background.

I began my cautious descent down the stairs, only taking one step at a time before stopping for a moment. My ears stayed sharp, listening for any disturbances from the master bedroom. I released a quick sigh of relief once I hit the floor of the hallway. Excitement tingled in my stomach as I drank in the thrill of sneaking around. It was a wild, heady feeling that took hold, like when Dad would go too fast down a country lane. I would always tighten my grip on the arm of the door, but the grin never left my face. It was that exact feeling of knowing it was dangerous and relishing in the excitement of it. And it had been so long since I had felt this.

My hand grazed the handle of the backdoor. I gave it a gentle tug and it creaked open. It was never locked.

A cold breeze greeted me, flushing my cheeks. I shoved my hood up, scraping my black hair with it to blend in with the fabric, and stepped into the garden. The security light flashed as soon as I was out the door. Luckily, it was only my room and the bathroom that looked upon the garden, and my parents were never disturbed by the security light. It was always me.

Small, swinging lanterns illuminated the night-washed greenery and spewed shadows across the ground. It looked dull, yet mysterious as the lights beckoned me to the end of the garden.

There was a tiny opening at the bottom of our fence where Teddy used to escape from. I smiled at the memories of Dad throwing me over the fence to catch him. For a Dachshund, he was surprisingly fast.

I sank to my knees, bending over to make the hole bigger. Mum hadn't had the heart to fill it back up since his passing. Dirt piled up on either side of me as I continued to scoop. It clung to my hands, my sleeves and my fingernails, making them the same dirty brown as my eyes.

After I felt the hole was big enough, I wiggled myself under the fence until I was on the other side. I quickly sprang to my feet. Brown stained my jacket and pyjama bottoms as I wiped away the excess dirt. Apprehension started to settle in the pit of my stomach. It was going to be hard to hide all of this.

Just chill out, I thought, taking a deep breath; it can easily be sorted tomorrow.

Voices erupted from beyond the chain linked fence, reminding me of the goal - to find a way in. My garden lights made the fence glow silver against the darkened landscape.

I began walking beside the fence, scanning from top to bottom for any signs of sabotage. But nothing looked out of place. It was always the same.

Symmetrical, silver poles lined up in perfect order, guarding this isolated woodland from human touch. I breathed a heavy sigh into the night after looping around a third time.

There was something I was missing. These people had found a way in, but it wasn't the straightforward way I had thought before. If they hadn't gone through it, that meant they had found a way either over or under it.

Grabbing my phone, I flicked the torch on and bent down to examine the bottom of the fence. A muted grey covered the ground beneath it, acting as a division between the two areas. I rapped my knuckles on the grey part. It was solid concrete. There was no way they could've gone under.

I stretched my legs while glancing at the top of my obstacle. The only way I could think they had gone over it would be with a ladder. Yet, they couldn't of possibly snuck one in. Farmer Brian's german shepherd, Nico, guarded the main entrance to this middle section, and he had a prestigious reputation of keeping his owner informed of trespassers.

The only other way to get here, apart from my garden, was through the overgrown, prickly shrubbery bordering our estate from Brian's land. I trudged over to the bushes, shining my torch in front, and found a gaping hole infested with broken twigs and footprints. They led towards the fence before stopping by a tree near the side of it.

I followed the tracks to their ending and circled the tree, searching for more

No more revealed themselves. Confused, I stalked over to the fence. The light from my torch illuminated more footprints that started a few metres away from the other side of the pickets. I took a step back and looked around in confusion. People had definitely been through this way and found a way over the fence, but how?

I glanced up, guiding my torch in the same direction. My eyes widened as a long, barren branch stretched out, like a skeletal hand reaching from its grave, towards the fence. The branch reached just shy of the fence's edge. I quickly rounded the tree and found a foothold that would allow me to climb to the lowest branch.

Taking a deep breath, I put my phone between my teeth, ensuring the camera torch was facing upwards, and bit down. My foot placed itself inside the hole and with a great heave, I pushed myself up into the tree.

The tree was more barren than its counterparts, looking strangely naked compared to the bushy shadows of leaves behind it. There were buds scattered across the branches. I could feel the tiny lumps beneath my hands as I climbed further up. But they were stagnant, refusing to bloom, leaving the tree to expose its shame for all to see.

Once I reached the point of where the branch I needed was, I got on my hands and knees and began crawling towards the fence. The branch shook gently beneath me, but held steady. It was quite chunky, so it supported my weight easily.

As I edged to the end of the branch, I knew I was going to have to stand and jump. My hands grasped another branch above me to steady myself as I stood. Wobbling slightly, I looked over the fence for the safest and easiest place to land. A pile of leaves caught my eye, a few metres away from the fence and where the footprints started again. That was my landing point.

It had been years since I had jumped out of trees. When I was little, I only felt adrenaline when I climbed to the highest point of the trees in the woodland and gazed upon the rolling hills and tiny houses that surrounded us, like a monarch surveying the beauty of their kingdom. This place had been my little kingdom, the one place I felt calm and free. But it was ripped from me, cordoned off and guarded by metal spikes. All I had left was the tiny glimpse of it I could catch from my window. Sometimes, when my head got too busy, I would stare at my lost kingdom for hours wistfully waiting to return, like Rapunzel yearning for her freedom from her tower window.

Now only fear gripped me. A fear of breaking something. A fear of impaling myself on the sharp spikes. A fear that this place had lost its magic and had become a shell of its own beauty and wonder.

Voices snapped me out of my paralysis. They had been quiet for a while, but were becoming louder. The voices were still unclear, but close by. I tampered down my fear, shoving it into the dark recesses of my mind, and forced myself to only focus on the leaves. Quickly putting my phone back into my jacket pocket, I propelled myself off the branch with all my strength.

I was flying for a moment. The spikes below me could do nothing to halt me, and as the cold breeze pushed against me, I laughed. It was a breathy laugh, but one full of genuine joy.

As fast as I had taken off, I descended to the ground before falling into the pile of leaves. My bottom throbbed, taking the whole of the impact of my crash landing. But I had made it, completed unscathed. My happy squeal echoed through the night before I clamped my hand over my mouth.

I was back. The breeze ruffled my flyaway hairs that had escaped during my descent. I took my bobble out and let the frizzy mess it was dance with the breeze. It blew harder against me and I giggled, feeling more welcomed than ever.

Even with the darkness robbing the woodland of its colour, I could still feel it was unchanged in the way I felt more at ease than I had in years.

The voices were now a whisper in the woods, but loud enough to catch my attention. I got to my feet and followed the whispers deeper into the woodland, where it became more overgrown and tangled with weeds and roots. I kept my phone safely trapped in my pocket, knowing I didn't need any light. This place would always keep me safe.

I was getting closer to the voices, but they were becoming quieter the nearer I got.

My fingers traced the greenery as I kept walking. The rough bark of trees. The prickles of a bush. The soft petals of some wildflower. Everything was the same. Nothing had crumbled and died.

An exposed root stopped me in my tracks as the voices vanished.

'Hello?' I whispered into the breeze. 'I'm sorry to disturb you, but I really wanted to come back here.'

Nobody answered. I took my phone from my pocket and turned the torch back on. A small area of grassland greeted me, but that wasn't what made me gasp. Old willow branches held together by string and zipties created a dome with an opening. Inside the dome lay tattered pillows, torn blankets and logs laid horizontally as seats. This was my home.

I had spent so many weeks during the summer of my eleventh year making a place that was all my own. And it was still here. Old and battered, but still here. I let out a choked sob and ran over to it.

It looked exactly the same as I had left it at the end of that summer before the fences had been put up. I think I had been in the middle of making a flower crown with mum's plastic flowers. They were strewn all over the ground in the dome. Dirty, dull and missing some petals, but I could still see the pinks, reds and purples they used to be.

To my side, a blue toy bunny sat looking into the wilderness.

'Fluffy,' I said, picking the teddy up. She had been my favourite teddy as a child. We used to always escape here and play. But I had forgotten her on that last day. I'd assumed that she had been thrown away accidentally by mum's annual summer clean out.

Her fur was grubby with dirt and age. One of her button eyes was missing and one floppy ear was hanging on by its last thread. Considering how long she'd been out in the woods, she was still surprisingly intact.

My eyes began to water as I hugged Fluffy close. I placed her on my lap and gathered the wayward flowers. The twine that would become my full crown lay beside me. Threading the flowers through it, I smiled as nostalgia washed over me. It was unchanged in this whole den, and it had survived against everything, including the passage of time. Once again, I was eleven years old and making a flower crown with my best friend.

DRIFTING

The cool breeze of summer nudged the canoe further into the lake. It rocked back and forth in gentle sways as the two girls stared at the blinding sun through tinted vision. They laid leisurely against the wooden seat, legs sprawled wide and tangled together, in comfortable silence. Only the sounds of the lapping water, quaking ducks and slight rustle of the trees that enclosed the lake filled the air.

'So this is it?' Phoebe said, turning towards Victoria, pushing the sunglasses onto her head and her wild chestnut curls back with it.

Her best friend put a hand over Phoebe's own in answer.

Phoebe understood the gesture. It was Victoria's little way of telling her to stop overthinking and be in the moment with her. Through their decade long friendship, that gesture had eased Phoebe many times when her brain tried to get too loud. Knowing that Victoria was by her side always helped in small ways.

Yet, looking at her friend soaking in the evening sun with no care in the world, her blonde hair glowing like burnished gold, tugged at Phoebe's heart. How long would it be until next time, she thought, trying to burn every little detail of this moment into her mind.

Victoria entwined their hands together before resting her head on Phoebe's bare shoulder.

Sighing in defeat, Phoebe turned back to the sun dipping towards the west and beginning to streak the sky in bright orange. It would be dark soon. The canoe would have to be brought in long before then. Victoria, the only one who knew how to row, would set their course for shore in an hour at the latest. Their time together was coming to an end. Tomorrow, Victoria would be heading on a plane to Germany to start university and Phoebe would remain in this little town, attending the local one.

Phoebe pushed their inevitable separation out of her head as she felt the soft squeeze of Victoria's hand. She put head against her friend's and squeezed back. At least they could enjoy one last sunset together.

FALLEN

A wave of agony rippled through my body as I drowsily tried to sit up. A sharp yelp echoed throughout the dank air. My body protested against my repeated attempts until I gave in and curled up on the hard ground. The pounding in my head grew, distorting my vision into a carousel of whirring greys and blacks. I screamed in frustration as fresh tears spilled out. I just wanted this to end. But every time I gathered the strength to try to get up, the pain reminded me I was too weak, too fragile, too worthless to leave.

'Hello?' The word reverberated around the enclosed walls. My sobs stopped. Someone was here. They could help me. Hope blossomed within my aching body. I spun my head around against the pounding pain, trying to find the identity of my saviour.

Sunlight burst from an opening high above me, where a shadowed figure sat on the edge with their legs dangling down. The light pooled into my surroundings, allowing me to see them properly for the first time. Jagged rock walls towered over me. I strained my neck trying to find where the walls ended, but they disappeared into the darkness far above the opening. Everywhere seemed to be cold and grim.

Yet, small spots of moss grew sporadically from the greying walls and ground. The sunlight glazed over certain patches, making them shine like tiny emeralds. My breath caught at the sight. It made this place seem more mystical, despite the bleakness.

'Are you okay down there?' The figure asked. Their voice was a soft whisper, but it still echoed into the deepness of my cage.

'I'm…stuck,' I replied hoarsely. I struggled to get the words out. The pain was making my mind a jumble. I shook my head, trying to stay focused on the opening.

Maybe I should just lie back down, I thought, this is too hard. I began to lower myself to the ground. The figure would go away, eventually.

'I can help you.' I rose slowly, fighting against my need to give in. The person chucked a rope from their ledge. It dropped, hitting the ground. My eyes widened as it swayed slowly to a stop. I pressed my hands into the ground and pushed myself up onto my legs. I bared my teeth, ignoring the objections of my tormented body.

There were only a few metres between me and the rope.

I took my first step before a sharp pain in my head forced me to cry out. Collapsing to my knees and holding my head against the floor, I whimpered.

'I…can't…can't get up,' I said through my gasping breaths. 'I'm not… strong enough.'

'That's okay, I'll wait for you here until you are.' I curled back up into my tiny ball, falling away into a restless slumber. 'I promise'

NO STRESS

The turquoise waters of the ocean lapped lazily at the white, sandy shores. Small waves rolled in as little fishing boats swayed rhythmically with them in the distance. My legs stretched out towards the horizon, basking in the evening sun. It was dipping low, teasing the sea with its distant embrace. Yet, they played with their colours. The sun painted the sky in a hazy amber while the sea reflected it back in soft watercolours.

Soon, a canvas of stars would replace it, signalling the end of my tranquility. In under twenty-four hours, I would be bound to a plane heading to London. I would resume the stressful life I had temporarily left behind.

I closed my eyes, focusing on the sound of the waves receding. It wasn't over yet. There was still time to relish in this paradise. Letting out a happy sigh, I reopened them drinking in the spectacular sunset.

ACKNOWLEDGEMENTS

There are many people I need to thank for their continued support and encouragement to pursue my writing.

To Jack, my amazing boyfriend, who has been my constant cheerleader and been there for me in some low moments over the last five years. This collection wouldn't have been possible without you. You've kept pushing me to do this even when I wanted to give up and read many drafts, even though you hate reading. You're my rock, keeping me steady in this crazy world.

To my mum, Leanne, I want to thank you for always believing in me and teaching me that I can achieve anything through handwork and commitment. You've given me so much, and I'm forever grateful for your love and support.

To my grandparents, Christine and Barry, you've supported this dream since I was a little girl and read all the silly stories I gave you. Without Taid's continuous questions of 'are you still writing?' and Nan's help during some periods of writer's block, I don't know how I would have started this.

To Anna, my editor, manager, proofreader, partner in crime, passenger princess, photographer, singing partner, and one of my closest and best friends (Is that enough titles?). Thank you for everything you have done for me. Without you, this collection would never have been finished. Thank you for helping me through edits, listening to incoherent rambles, talking me through moments of self-doubt and, most importantly, always being there. You're my guiding star.

Also shout out to my brother, Liam, who only wants me to keep writing because he wants to star in a film someday.

Thank you to the editors of Pandora's Inbox, where the following pieces have appeared: 'Call of the Woods', 'Long Journey Home', 'Mark of Victory', 'Déjà vu', 'Eirene' and 'Drifting'.

Thank you to the editors of 101 Words, where the following piece has appeared: 'Snow Fall'.

Thank you to the editors of The Drabble, where the following piece has appeared: 'The Fox in the City'.

Thank you to the editors of Your Fire Magazine, where the following piece has appeared: 'On the Doorstep'.

ABOUT THE AUTHOR

SHANNON JAMES

Shannon James was born and raised in the countryside between the borders of England and Wales. This is where her love of nature, daydreams and magic began and inspired her journey into writing. Her work has been published in several online magazines, such as Pandora's Inbox and The Drabble. While Shannon enjoys going on adventures around the world and in books, she can often be found either sleeping, playing The Sims or re-watching her favourite sitcoms. She continues to live in the countryside with her boyfriend, very large family and adorable dog, Bandit. You can visit her at https://shannonjamesauthor.weebly.com or follow her on Instagram at @shannonjamesauthor.

Printed in Great Britain
by Amazon